SITTING
IN MY BOX

for Brett,
who remembers sitting in his box
D. L.

PUFFIN BOOKS

Published by the Penguin Group
Penguin Books USA Inc., 375 Hudson Street, New York, New York 10014, U.S.A.
Penguin Books Ltd, 27 Wrights Lane, London W8 5TZ, England
Penguin Books Australia Ltd, Ringwood, Victoria, Australia
Penguin Books Canada Ltd, 10 Alcorn Avenue, Toronto, Ontario, Canada M4V 3B2
Penguin Books (N.Z.) Ltd, 182-190 Wairau Road, Auckland 10, New Zealand

Penguin Books Ltd, Registered Offices: Harmondsworth, Middlesex, England

Library of Congress number 89-31609
ISBN 0-14-054819-X

Published in the United States by Dutton Children's Books,
a division of Penguin Books USA Inc.
375 Hudson Street, New York, New York 10014

Designer: Barbara Powderly

Printed in Hong Kong by South China Printing Co.
First Unicorn Edition 1992
10 9 8 7 6 5 4 3 2 1

A Puffin Unicorn

DUTTON CHILDREN'S BOOKS
NEW YORK

SITTING
IN MY BOX

by DEE LILLEGARD
pictures by JON AGEE

Sitting in my box.

A tall giraffe knocks.

"Let me, let me in."
So I move over.

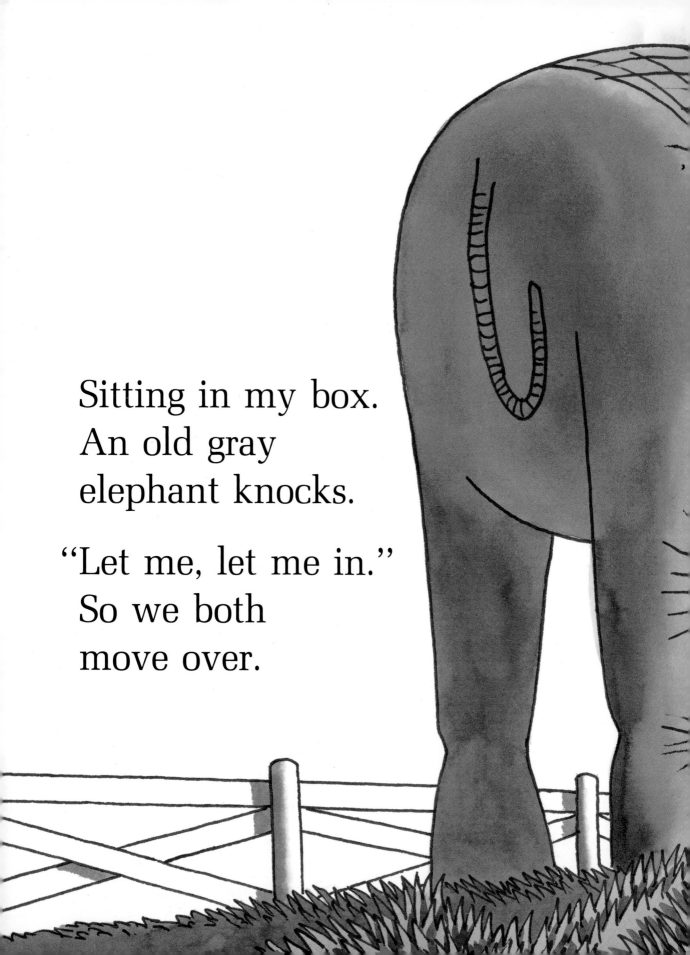

Sitting in my box.
An old gray
elephant knocks.

"Let me, let me in."
So we both
move over.

Sitting in my box.
A big baboon knocks.

"Let me, let me in."
So we all move over.

Sitting in my box.
A grumpy lion knocks.

"Let me, let me in."
So we all move over.

Sitting in my box.
A hippopotamus knocks.

"Let me, let me in."
So we *all* move over.

Standing in my box.
There's no room to sit.

"Wait a minute!
This box has
too much in it."

"Someone has to go."

"Not me."

"Not me."

"Not me."

"Not me."

"Not me."

Sitting in my box.
Along comes a flea.
A flea *never* knocks.
He jumps right in.

He bites the hippo
and the grumpy lion.

He bites the baboon
and the old gray
elephant.

He bites the tall giraffe.

That's why I'm
sitting in my box...

just me.